THE WEE PUPPY

WHO WOULDN'T GO TO SLEEP

A Grosset & Dunlap **ALL ABOARD BOOK**™

To Art Evans, who never wanted to go to sleep — J.B.M.

For Laurel Eugenia — K.L.S.

THE WEE PUPPY
WHO WOULDN'T GO TO SLEEP

By Jane B. Mason
Illustrated by Karen Lee Schmidt

Grosset & Dunlap, Publishers

It was bedtime for Wee Puppy.

"Let's pick up your toys and get you into your pajamas," said Papa Dog.

But Wee Puppy did *not* want to go to bed.

"I'm not tired," he said. "I want to stay up and play."

"Tomorrow is going to be a big day," Papa Dog answered. "It's Wee Kitten's birthday party. And you need your rest." And he marched Wee Puppy upstairs.

In Wee Puppy's room, Papa Dog read Wee Puppy a bedtime story. But before he could finish the last sentence, Wee Puppy was choosing another book from his shelf.

"Read me another story," he begged.

Papa Dog shook his head. "It's time for you to close your eyes and go to sleep." He tucked the covers around Wee Puppy and gave him a kiss good night.

But Wee Puppy did not want to close his eyes. Not one tiny bit. He could hear Mama Dog in the kitchen and wondered what she was doing.

He crept down the stairs. Soon Wee Puppy was standing in the kitchen doorway.

"Mama," he said, "I forgot to go to the bathroom. And it's dark in the hallway."

So Mama Dog turned on the hallway light and waited while Wee Puppy went to the bathroom. Then she tucked him back into bed.

But Wee Puppy did not stay in bed for very long.

Mama and Papa Dog were watching the news when they heard the pitter-patter of little paws.

"Mama," sniffled Wee Puppy as he came into the living room, "I have a boo-boo. Will you kiss it and make it better?"

Mama Dog leaned over and kissed Wee Puppy's paw.

"It still hurts," Wee Puppy whimpered. "Maybe if I watch TV with you it will feel better."

"You can watch TV another time," Mama Dog
replied. "Right now you need to go to sleep."
And she sent Wee Puppy upstairs *again*.

But Wee Puppy just couldn't fall alseep, no matter how hard he tried. And so much later, when Mama and Papa Dog came upstairs, they heard a voice call out from Wee Puppy's room.

"Mama, Papa, I have to tell you something."

"What is it?" Papa Dog asked.

"I'm not sleepy," Wee Puppy said.

Mama and Papa Dog came into Wee Puppy's room. "It is late, and little puppies should be sound asleep," Mama Dog said as she smoothed Wee Puppy's ears. "Now close your eyes and go to sleep."

Then Mama and Papa Dog kissed Wee Puppy good night again and went to sleep.

But not Wee Puppy! As soon as Mama and Papa Dog turned out their light, Wee Puppy tiptoed downstairs.

Maybe I'll have a little snack, thought Wee Puppy. So he filled a plate with his favorite cookies—chewy chocolate chip— and he poured himself a big glass of milk. He put everything on a tray and carried it into the living room.

Maybe I'll watch some TV, thought Wee Puppy. So first he watched a little bit of news.

Then he watched an old, old movie.

Then he flipped to a station where they talked in a different language.

Finally he found the channel with cartoons. He watched that channel until all the cookies were gone and his glass of milk was empty.

Soon Wee Puppy's eyelids were drooping and he decided to go back upstairs.

Maybe I'll read a story, thought Wee Puppy. So he pulled a book off his bookshelf and began to read. But before he had even turned the first page, Wee Puppy's mouth opened in a giant yawn.

"I'm not sleepy at all," he told himself as he carried the book to bed. But his eyes were feeling very heavy, and before long they were closed.

"Time to wake up, little one. It's going to be a big day," said Mama Dog the next morning. She raised the shade in Wee Puppy's room.

Wee Puppy opened one eye—slowly.

"It's almost time for breakfast," Mama Dog said. "We're making your favorite—blueberry pancakes."

At breakfast, Wee Puppy yawned between almost every bite. His pancakes did not taste so good, and his tummy felt a little funny. Maybe it hadn't been such a good idea to eat all those cookies the night before.

When breakfast was over, Wee Puppy and Papa Dog wrapped Wee Kitten's present. But Wee Puppy was so tired that his paw kept slipping off the package each time Papa Dog tried to tie the bow.

At last it was time to go to Wee Kitten's party. Wee Puppy kissed his parents good-bye and walked down the path to Wee Kitten's house.

He could hardly wait to see all of his friends. But it seemed like the path went on forever. Wee Puppy dragged his tired little paws, and by the time he reached the party, he was just a little grumpy.

Wee Puppy's friends were all at the party: Wee Piggy, Wee Bunny, Wee Lamb, Wee Ducky, and of course, Wee Kitten. They were all having fun playing games.

"Wee Puppy!" they called to him. "Come play with us."

First they played Duck, Duck, Goose. But Wee Puppy wasn't having much fun. He had to be the goose over and over again. He was so tired that he couldn't catch anyone—not even Wee Lamb, who was practically a baby!

Wee Puppy decided he was sick of Duck, Duck, Goose. And all of a sudden, he burst into tears. This birthday party was no fun at all!

"I want to go home," he whimpered. So Mama Cat called Mama Dog and she came to get Wee Puppy. They left just as everyone else sat down to eat big pieces of cake.

On the way home, Mama Dog asked Wee Puppy what was wrong. Wee Puppy told Mama Dog about staying up late the night before. He even told her about the cookies.

"Now do you see why little puppies need their sleep at night?" Mama Dog asked gently. "It's so they'll have lots of energy to do fun things during the day."

That night, Wee Puppy could hardly wait for bedtime.

"Do you want a story?" Papa Dog asked after Wee Puppy had put on his pajamas.

"No, thanks," Wee Puppy answered. Then he snuggled under the covers and thought about all the things he would do the next day. Before long, Wee Puppy was fast asleep.